MOVE YOUR MOOD!

by Brenda S. Miles, PhD, and
Colleen A. Patterson, MA

illustrated by Holly Clifton-Brown

Magination Press • Washington, DC
American Psychological Association

Feeling blah? Here's what to do.

MOVE YOUR BODY

and your mood moves too!

TWIST OUT TIRED!

Twist. Twist. Twist.

Wiggle like this!

FLY aWaY FeaRFUL.

Fly. Fly. Fly.

Bye. Bye. Bye.

SHAKE AWAY STUBBORN.

Shakety-shake-shake.

GROWL
aWaY GRUMPY!

Grr-Grr-Grrreat!

HOP TO HAPPY!

Hop. Hop. Hop.

Feeling better?
No time to stop!

MARCH FOR MOTiVaTeD.

March, march, NOW!

Waddle, waddle, WOW!

CLAP FOR CONFIDENT.

Clap, clap, hooray!

NOW POSE
FOR PROUD.

Today's your day!

STRETCH YOUR SMILE!

Stretch it W-I-D-E.

WIGGLE

fly

WAVE

TWIST

CLAP

WADDLE

GROWL

SMILE SHAKE

HOP

POSE

MARCH

Do all the moves!
Feel great inside!

NoTe To PaReNTs, CaReGiVeRs, aND TeaCHeRs

Children experience a range of emotions. For parents, caregivers, and teachers, this statement is not surprising. Sometimes a child is quiet and contented, other times angry and frustrated. Often the time between one emotion and the next is quite short. Big swings in emotions—with little warning and no obvious triggers—are a normal part of childhood.

Young brains struggle to regulate feelings. Adult brains struggle, too, but we have learned to label our emotions, understand their triggers, and choose appropriate strategies—most of the time, hopefully—to help us feel better. For many adults, exercise is an effective way to elevate mood while keeping the body healthy. New research suggests that physical activity can help children feel better, too!

HoW To use THis Book

Ready to move your mood? Try using this book in the morning to start your day off in a good mood. For adults and children, it can be tough to get started in the morning. Research shows that when children are active their brains are more focused and ready to learn. At home, start your day with *Move Your Mood!* and energize your child for work and play. Teachers can use this book to start the day, too—during circle time or before morning seatwork—and again in the afternoon to re-energize and refocus the class.

Remember that activity boosts energy levels. So *Move Your Mood!* is best suited for the beginning or middle of the day—and perhaps right before homework once the school day is done. At bedtime, the key is to encourage your child to be calm and relaxed rather than excited and energetic. Quiet activities, like reading a book or listening to soft music, help to promote relaxation. As part of the bedtime routine, create some calming verses for a story of your own—for example, you could write rhymes like "Tiptoe to dreamland, hush, hush, hush. Snuggle in blankets, plush, plush, plush."

When energy is the goal, encourage large muscle movements as you and your child read this book. Exaggerated actions, large muscle movements, and big voices should help to create a positive mood and a sense of fun. Encourage children with restricted physical movements or disabilities to participate in any way they can. Waving, smiling, and cheering are all great options for being involved. Depending on a child's physical condition, and with medical approval, an adult may be able to dance with a child in a wheelchair through gentle movements. Make sure there is adequate room for everyone to move without any objects or hazards getting in the way.

MoRe iDeas FoR MoViNG YouR MooD

Reading this book with your child and moving together are fun ways to link actions—and eventually exercise—with feeling better. Here are more ideas for teaching children about emotions and how moving can boost mood.

Write more verses. Invite children to be part of the creative process by inventing their own action-emotion pairings. Encourage children to think "outside the book" and write new verses. To get started, ask children to show you what actions they enjoy doing and to describe how those actions make them feel. Talk about the emotion words that might work best to label those feelings. Encourage children to consider a range of emotions and a variety of actions. The possibilities are endless, so support high-energy brainstorming! For an added challenge, try to think of actions and emotions that start with the same letter—just like in the book! "Dance to determined," "jog away jealous," "bounce to better," and "jump for joy" are some examples. Be sure to include your new verses the next time you read *Move Your Mood!*

Label feelings. Children who understand emotion labels and recognize many different feelings have a good foundation for friendships and empathy. *Move Your Mood!* covers a wide range of emotions. Use the verses in the book, and any new ones you create, as part of a larger discussion about feelings. You can help to develop these skills, too, by creating an "emotion dictionary." Generate emotion labels and pair them with photographs of facial expressions for emotions such as grumpy, happy, and confident. Your child could even model the facial expressions! Some children may also have fun drawing the facial expressions and displaying their pictures in an "emotion gallery."

Use more words to come up with more solutions. In times of upset, children with a limited "emotion vocabulary" may describe themselves as "mad" or "sad" and react accordingly with aggression or crying. These basic terms may not describe accurately what children are feeling, and imprecision makes finding solutions difficult for children, parents, and teachers. When children begin to use a richer emotion vocabulary, adults and children are better able to generate appropriate solutions that target specific moods. For example, a child who is "mad" may throw a printing worksheet on the floor. However, a child who is "frustrated" may see the benefit of asking for help or trying alternate solutions, like writing big letters on a board instead of using a pencil and paper. Positive emotions also deserve to be understood in all of their variations. When children move beyond basic labels like "happy" to more specific terms like "proud," "confident," and "motivated," they gain a better sense of these feelings and the various routes to achieving them. Be sure to describe your own emotions with a range of feeling words so that children can hear and see your impressive emotion vocabulary in action!

Remember that all emotions are okay. Everyone feels a range of emotions—from happy to sad, from angry to excited. Teach your child that all emotions are okay and that everyone experiences a range of feelings in different situations, even parents and teachers! Feelings are never a problem, but sometimes our response to those feelings can be upsetting and hurtful. Explain that if you feel angry and hit someone, the action is the problem, not the feeling behind it. Encourage children to use their emotion labels and share their feelings with words. Explain that "moving your mood" does not mean using actions to hurt other people, like kicking, punching, or biting. Moving your mood means moving your own body in your own space to feel better.

Be a mover, too. Children model what they see. In adults, exercise promotes physical health, and mental health, too. Be an inspiring role model and aim to stay active. Participate in activities with your child without competitive expectations. For example, you can go for a walk with your child or throw some hoops together. Discuss openly how moods can be moved by talking about them and by moving your body, too.

Move Your Mood! is not a substitute for regular medical care. If low mood or a high level of worry persists, consult your child's doctor or mental health professional. If statements of self-harm are made, go to your nearest hospital emergency room. As with any exercise program, consult your child's doctor prior to starting.

For Joanne, a fabulous friend and marvelous mood booster—BSM
For my parents who are always encouraging and supportive—CAP
For Jazzy & Amberly—HC-B

Published by
MAGINATION PRESS ®
An Educational Publishing Foundation Book
American Psychological Association
750 First Street NE
Washington, DC 20002

Magination Press is a registered trademark of the American Psychological Association.

For more information about our books, including a complete catalog, please write to us, call 1-800-374-2721, or visit our website at www.apa.org/pubs/magination.

Book design by Sandra Kimbell
Printed by Phoenix Color Corporation, Hagerstown, MD

Library of Congress Cataloging-in-Publication Data

Names: Miles, Brenda. | Patterson, Colleen A. | Clifton-Brown, Holly, illustrator.
Title: Move your mood! : Brenda S. Miles, PhD and Colleen A. Patterson, MA ; illustrated by Holly Clifton-Brown.
Description: Washington, DC : Magination Press, [2016] | "American Psychological Association." | Summary: "Provides a fun active way to learn about emotions, linking movement with mood"— Provided by publisher.
Identifiers: LCCN 2015014374| ISBN 9781433821127 (hardcover) | ISBN 1433821125 (hardcover)
Subjects: | CYAC: Emotions—Fiction. | Human body—Fiction. | Mood (Psychology)—Fiction.
Classification: LCC PZ7.M5942 Mo 2016 | DDC [E]—dc23 LC record available at http://lccn.loc.gov/2015014374

Manufactured in the United States of America
First printing January 2016
10 9 8 7 6 5 4 3 2 1